Treasure Hunting

101

A step by step guide to be successful finding gold,

treasure, and other valuables

By Matthew Williams

Contents

A Fair Warning!

Treasure, it's everywhere you look. It's here, it's

there. It's rounds, it's square and most never dare.

Ok enough with this Dr. Seuss bull crap people.

Treasure hunting is serious shit and if you're

reading this book you have come to the right place

the get the inside scoop! Within this book lie the

deepest, darkest, most vital tips to finding treasure

which have been guarded by the Treasure Hunters

Alliance for centuries. I have dedicated my life to

treasure hunting and have traveled the globe in

dedication to treasure hunting. I have reaped the

fruits of my labors and now it's time for me to give

back to all you schmucks who don't know what

you're doing out there. Well get your notebook,

your highlighter and put on a pair of depends

because you're not going to stop reading this book

until it's finished and even then you're probably not

going to want to do anything but plan your next

treasure adventure!

First off I must warn you about the contents of

this book and the responsibilities you will hold in

learning the information. This book will teach you

things the Treasure Hunter Alliance will not want

you to know. If one of these member's catch you

reading this book and its secrets you will not only

never be able to join the alliance but some of the

crazier members may even try to break your legs!

Some of the alliance members have paid off book

store cashiers to keep an eye out for buyers of this

book where when they see someone buy the book

they make a call... Some instances even show book

store cashiers putting trackers on the book when

you buy it so you can be tracked by the alliance. For

your sake I hope you bought it off the internet and

shipped it to a P.O. box. If you didn't I simply warn

you to keep your eyes out and watch your back for the alliance.

In this book you won't see proper grammar, spelling or book writing. We're treasure hunters, we aint got time for that! This book gets straight to the point and I need to publish it before the alliance finds me so there won't even be a proof reader. Grammar is important but treasure is importanter.

What is Treasure?

Basically anything valuable that someone will

pay you for. Although we talk to gold and finding

gold a lot that's just because it's the most common

for treasure hunters weather it's raw or you're

finding gold Persian coins but there are many, many

9

types of treasure. Diamonds are great finds but usually only for very specific areas and if you are familiar with the movie blood diamond you know it's a bloody business. I have never specialized in trying to find raw diamonds in my treasure hunting. Unlike my desire to find raw gold I would rather find diamonds in jewelry. Early in my treasure hunting career before I hit it big, I wasted 6 months of my life at a dig site finding tons of diamonds! Then when I ran out of money and had dug my heart out I went to cash them in only to find they were crystals

and cubic zirconia gems. What a load of crock! All

my crystals only added up to getting me 45 bucks

and a used Gameboy. After that I went into a deep

depression and then spent the next 2 years of my

life trying to "hack the matrix" with no success.

Follow my example and be careful hunting for

diamonds.

Ancient scrolls are great finds since all these

history buffs and museums will want a piece of the

goods. Soon as a museum, an institution, or

someone from the gold market (like the black

market but for treasure) low balls you for your

ancient scrolls just pull up facetime, call your friend

and have them hold a lighter next to the scrolls.

95% of the time they cave and give you the money

you want but if they absolutely won't cave have

your friend start burning them. Now they will cave

as they watch it burn and if they don't then hey,

burn all of it and keep it real. Nobody intimidates

us, we're treasure hunters.

Fallout shelters will be talked to later but these

are obvious treasure finds and are like triple prizes.

You get a new man cave for your bros, a fallout

shelter for your family and it will up the value of

your residence tenfold! Do you know how many

weirdos out there are dooms day preppers and will

pay top dollar for a fallout shelter. Through

extensive research and my relator Jerry, he says

that houses have been reported to have quadrupled in value when a fallout shelter is found! The crazier this world gets, the more we make fun of Kim Jong-un and his fat face the more your fallout shelter is worth. Kim Jong-un is a tard. See I literally just increased value of all fallout shelters when his servants report that sentence to him. You're welcome people.

Watches and antiques are very commonly found in houses that past generations lived in and you are the first to buy. They are also very common in your grandma's basement. I spend hours and hours researching the antique roadshow and watching how much these antiques are worth. I then go to my grandma's house and search for treasure. What your family considers a normal visit to grandma's house will now be an exciting treasure hunt full of mystery and valuables. Now when you do find the goods you will have to know the right ways to ask for it. Bake granny a pie, color them a picture or maybe it's as simple as mowing their lawn but be sure you ask before you take. I simply tell granny were going to get some stuff appraised and split it 50/50. When I took in my grandma's Patek Philippe pocket watch which was valued at 1.5 million it shocked us both! We cashed in on the spot for 1.3 million! I spent my money investing in 3 locations of Motel 6 which tanked but grandma got herself that Cadillac and moved to a place where the beer flows like wine and beautiful women instinctively flock like the salmon of Capistrano. A little place called Aspen, Colorado. Treasure is in the eyes of the beholder but I'm not in it for the liberal, hippy, meaningful bull crap some call treasure. I'm in it to win it baby. Sure I spent over half a million on Motel 6 chains that went under but there's plenty of treasure to be found and other things to invest in like the Super 8 Hotel chain!

Right Under Your Nose

Did you know you may be sitting on a gold mine? Did you know 15% of people bury random treasure in their backyards for a rainy day? Let me tell you why your own backyard may just be a treasure pit. The Gold Reserve Act of 1934 outlawed most private possession of gold, forcing individuals

to sell it to the Treasury, after which it was stored in

United States Bullion Depository at Fort Knox and

other locations. A year earlier, in 1933, Executive

Order 6102 had made it a criminal offense for U.S.

citizens to own or trade gold anywhere in the world,

with exceptions for some jewelry and collector's

coins. These prohibitions were relaxed starting in

1964 – gold certificates were again allowed for

private investors on April 24, 1964, although the

obligation to pay the certificate holder on demand

in gold specie would not be honored. By 1975

Americans could again freely own and trade gold.

So you think you're free in America? Think again,

the government loves to get their share of the

goods just as much as us treasure hunters,

especially that pizza face, Franklin Delano Roosevelt

who wanted all of it! What would I do if the

government wanted to enact a bunch of liberal bull

crap and take my guns? I would put them in a case

or chest and bury them 3-6 ft into the ground! Well

that's what all our great and great great

grandparents did in 1934. With gold owning not

calming down until the 1960 (thank you Jimi

Hendrix) much of that gold was forgotten or people

passes away while all their treasure is still out there.

Many people would bury this stuff without even

telling their families where it was out so even their

family couldn't cave under the questioning of the

government while they were interrogated with

jumper cables hooked to their nipples. Google it

and you will see just how many people stumble

across huge finds of treasure in their yards! Just to

be clear, Google treasure finds in people's

backyards, not jumper cable nipple torture you sick

freaks. One couple for example in California found a

can slightly sticking out of the ground along a trail

they had walked for years. He dug it out of the

ground and in the can were gold coins valued at

over 10 million dollars! They weren't even trying,

they didn't have a metal detector or nothing and

now they're rich! They used to make a living making

shirts for people in Hawaii, now they party in Hawaii

24/7! This is just one example to show you it can be

right under your nose.

Old people are your best friends! It's very

common they don't trust banks, they don't trust the

stock market and they save everything for a rainy

day. But what happens is we use that damn

antiperspirant all our lives, develop dementia, and

forget about our stored away treasure. We don't

hide it in a safe (unless that safe is hidden). The next

time you move into a new house I want you

searching the yard, the attic and the crawl spaces.

It's here you're going to get the easy wins whether

it's cash, guns, gold, jewelry, watches or maybe

even a secret fallout shelter from the cold war era! I

don't know any guy who wouldn't consider a fallout

shelter one of the best treasures finds. Just imagine

turning it into a real man cave. Have guns hanging

on the walls like spy movies and break out the N64, this is why buying older vintage houses are worth it. I always research as much as I can to who lived at a house before I buy it. If they worked for FBI or CIA then jackpot! But if they worked at the local scrap yard you're more likely to find a hidden can of beans for a rainy day over a badass fallout shelter. These are all things to consider when purchasing a new home.

You can also be your best friend when it comes to treasure. You have treasure inside you right now! It's called a kidney and after I wasted 2 years trying to hack the matrix I was out of money and in debt 45K. I needed a way out and I needed some start up cash. I needed some insider information so I moved to Las Vegas. I was starting to make a living after I read a book by Anthony Crafts on how to play slot machines. It's a guide to improving overall chances of winning and it got my life back on track. I highly recommend this book which can be found on

Amazon. But the slots isn't where I was getting my

inside information, it was at the blackjack tables. I

was a blackjack dealer and learned everything you

needed to know on how to make quick cash. You

sell your organs on the black market! There are

always millionaires out there who need them and

are willing to fork out serious "treasure" for a good

healthy one. You will need to find your own ways

here but basically I got in with the local Chinese

Triad gangs and their hook ups. I met the doctor

and even spoke with some of the past clients for

their testimony on the procedure. Basically they fly

you the Philippines, put you in a 5 star hotel, do the

surgery and fly you home. They usually keep you in

the 5 star hotel with full amenities for 7 days to

recover enough to fly you home. When you get

home you have your money deposited in your

offshore account. Everyone's deal is different but I

insured I got top dollar buy watching a Pawn Stars

marathon to insure I had proper training to

negotiate the deal. For reference I ended up with

425K, if you don't call that treasure than stop

reading this book now, buy the book I referenced

on slot machines and make a living that way.

Treasure hunting is not for you if you won't even

sell your kidney. With this money I was able to

acquire all my equipment I needed to gets started

and pay off my debts with the Triad.

Connecting the Dots Through Movies

One great resource for research on treasure are

movies. In this chapter we will examine a few

example of how you can use movies to not only

enjoy and motivate but to also use as research.

For example let's look at one of the biggest

treasure finds in movies, The Count of Monte

Cristo. According to google this movie was filmed

largely in the Malta area. Blue Lagoon, Dwejra

and Crystal Lagoon to name just a few. Now we

already know places to sail and scuba dive to find

the goods! If you're into sailing you have a huge

advantage as less than 1% of treasure finder's sail

since they are to poor sinking all their money into

the never-ending gamble of treasure hunting...

Now you can take the family on vacation "which

we will be talking about later" while you look for

treasure! Usually treasure hunters like me who

have a sail boat are hunters who have already

struck it rich and then go out and invest in more

ways to find even more treasure! You can also

find many other clues in movies on where to find

treasure like in the movie 300. Remember when

the rich Persians were sailing their troops over to

Sparta to takeover for king Xerxes? Well if you

have seen the show you know there was a big

storm wrecking those ships into the cliffs and

sinking them! We also know king Xerxes treated

himself as a god and wore only the best and finest

gold so we know there was a tremendous amount

of gold on those ships. Now the movie doesn't say

where those cliffs are but let's go through what

we know. Sparta, also known as **Lacedaemon**,

was an ancient Greek city-state located primarily

in the present-day region of southern **Greece**

called **Laconia**. Now I'm not going to tell you

where exactly to go but with a bit of research on google, google earth and re-watching the ship wreck scene in the movie I trust you can find it.

Me and my good friend Pablo Antonio got the easy stuff but we know there is still plenty hidden in the sands and washed around the area.

Whenever we start running low on treasure we meet up and usually find over 1 million worth in bounty within a weeks' time and you can too if you invest enough time and research! Just to be clear this is a secret straight from Pablo and I that

even the Treasure Hunters Alliance doesn't know

about.

   While we are on the subject of sailing, diving

and oceans let also take a look at Titanic. In this

movie we meet one of the most selfish woman in

history, Rose. In the movie we listen to Rose take

us through her adventure of being a spoiled rich

girl on the Titanic. With being spoiled and rich she

also owns one of the most sought after diamonds

in the world named "The Heart of the Ocean". My buddies and fellow treasure adventurer crew "Blue Steal" is the team leading the exploration in the Titanic movie. They haul Roses ass around spending millions in materials, crew members, resources and fuel to wonder the ocean in search to find the diamond on the Titanic. They never find it, Rose with her selfish greed had it all along! Instead of telling them to stop wasting their time, she hops aboard, waists their gas and resources only to throw that damn thing back in the ocean!

What a bitch! Now that treasure is down there

just waiting. Now just to clear up any confusion

the Heart of the Ocean diamond (which they say

has been found and auctioned off at 25 million) is

a fake. After the movie, French diamond makers

trained by Pierre LaDuche, made a replica and

passed it as the real thing. Now that diamond is

still worth a ton and is currently valued at 250

million but when you find the real thing just think

about how much it will be worth! Maybe over 500

million! Now according to the movie they have

now left the Titanic and are sailing at 30-35 knots

for 11-11.5 hours in a SWS direction. Now take

the coordinates of the shipwreck (**41.726931°** N

and **-49.948253°** W) and sail an average of 32.5

knots for 11.25 hours and stop. Now build a basic

treasure diamond radius of 5 miles in all

directions and you have your location. I share this

freely because this is no secret but with that

much ocean floor to be searching it's still been

undiscovered. Who knows, maybe Moby Dick

gobbled that bad boy up and pooped it out near

Jamaica! But the point I am here to make is that

movies are a very reliable source for information

to find your treasure and help steer your life

choices. I may have not found that damn diamond

the one time I tried but I did find some of that

Persian gold.

Now insure you keep in mind, not all movies are

a good reference for finding treasure. Just look at

those dipsticks in the Disney movie "Holes". These

turds are horrible at finding treasure! I do

however love their dedication and techniques in

finding legal ways to use child labor though.

Basically what they do is have kids who are in a

juvenile prison camp dig holes all day looking for

the goods. Every day they go to where some

treasure is supposedly buried and dig a hole 5

feet wide by 5 feet deep. After they have dug

their hole they get to go back to the prison yard

for kids where they're all slingin' pokemon cards

and bubblegum cigarettes. This is a horrible way

to find the treasure (which by luck they do end up

finding) when all they should have done is

invested in metal detectors! Hell if you can't

afford top notch metal detectors have the kids do

something to bring in cash to the camp which you

use for grade AAA metal detectors. In this movie

sure, they find the treasure but only by luck and a time period of many, many years and borderline legalities of child labor. Don't follow their example.

The last movie we need to mention is "The Goonies" and we should take them as the perfect example. They searched their attic, found a map and got their hands dirty. Within 24 hours of finding that map they found the goods. This was largely contributed to Sloth which reminds me to tell you it's always great to have some muscle on

your crew. Usually these meat heads are easily

manipulated with things like steak, salami,

pepperoni, hoagies and creatine. Or in Sloths

case, Baby Ruth candy bars. They kept this

meathead with them to do all the fighting and

heavy lifting and in the end for what? A Baby

Ruth! Now that's cheap labor and examples like

this should be a great learning opportunity for us.

By the end of The Goonies documentary these

little 12yr old turds find one eyed willies treasure

and if you do your research you will find that

these 12 year old turds actually started and still

own the Chuckie Cheese franchises to this day. If

a bunch of little pizza faced, prima donna, whiney

little turds can do it, so can you!

So Where Do We Find This Shit?

In this chapter we will take a deep look into

where geographically we have the best success

as treasure hunters. The Treasure Hunter

Alliance would have me lynched for this so and

most everything else in this book where I'm

talking about the deepest secrets in treasure

hunting but I already found my booty and am

retired. I will be liquidating all my assets and

living the rest of my days on private islands with

offshore accounts. But since I have my life all

lined up to live happy and safe from the alliance

I figured I would write this book showing the

secrets of my chronicling rise to power!

Gold and treasure have hotspots just like oil

does. You don't just find oil everywhere but you

can find some in just about every country. But

were not going to start up an oil rig in the

amazon jungle. That's where you go for wood

and paper... No we want to start our oil rig up

where the gold flows like wine. Like how the oil

flows in the desert lands of Saudi Arabia. Before

they knew they were sitting on the world's

largest "gold mine" of oil let's face it, it was a

dump. Now take a look at cities like Dubai, they do whatever they want will all the money! That's going to be you in 1-60 years if you follow this book and have just a little luck.

Our First huge destination for gold and treasure is Australia. Australia accounts for a huge amount of gold mined in the world but we're just ordinary people who don't have all the fancy mining gear. We have shovels, metal detectors and pans. We're going to find that gold the old school way, no middle man taxing

us up the didgeridoo, having to pay a crew of

hundreds while offering benefits and trying to

keep their candy ass's happy and engaged. No,

were out for the gold on a solo mission. It's just

us, naked, in nature, screaming out our gold

mating call to the wild and the gold is screaming

back. Can you hear it? Of course you can or you

wouldn't be reading this book. Now to business

and the secrets of Australia nobody wants you

to know. Look at southern Australia and you will notice all the gold mines are dead center where you will also still find big bodies of water. If you know anything about gold you know gold concentrates where water has pushed it or used to with ancient rivers that may be dried up now. Later we will hit on Southern Africa but now it's all starting to make sense. Gravity pulls water down and all these countries have all their largest gold deposits south of the country... You want the gold, go south! Now all these mines in southern Australia didn't account for the solo hunters like us out to get their gold. Look where the mines are, look where rivers (or ancient rivers) are flowing into the mines area and go up stream! For example look up the Terramin mine area. Now look how many rivers are just north or north-east. My third biggest find was a nugget off one of these rivers but I will refrain from the name out of respect for my old river partner, Edmond Dantes who still goes back to that area quit frequently. Also if I get any more specific the Terramin Angels will be after me. The Terramin Angels are a gold mining biker crew who will beat your ass with gold chains if you cross them. In fact don't even try to research or google them because they will search your IP address and pumble your ass. Ok enough about ass's, the real danger of treasure hunting in Australia are the kangaroos.

Especially around the mining area, kangaroos have been bread beat up and capture gold mining soloists like you and me. My advice is to do all treasure hunting in a top notch kangaroo suit so you look like one of them. This has seemed to do the trick for me and Desmond.

Now I do hear rumors they are experimenting with koala bears but their research shows they are still at least 5 years out from now or about 2022.

Next we need to address South Africa which

is where 40% of all gold mined in the world has

come from. The US geological survey estimates

that South Africa retains nearly 50% of the

world's UNMINED gold! Johannesburg is sitting

on top of the biggest gold basin ever

discovered! And where was this gold? In the

south since gravity pulled it down! Currently

many of the most predominant mines are

abandoned due to a massive industrial decline.

So what you're telling me is a bunch of bozos

have already dug the mine, where they find

tons "literally" of gold and then they left? Sign

me up! Now the first thing you need to do is

research the area for rival gangs and miners.

There are a lot of gold gangs and rival miners

that will shoot your ass for stepping foot in their

mine. I simply write about the Johannesburg

mines to educate you on the potential but I

personally have always avoided them. If I was

going to plan a dig there I first would study the

Rambo movies. Rambo 1-4 can show and teach

you what to do in the most extreme situations.

Rambo training is only to fall back on but first I

suggest talking to other treasure finders that

search the area and get in tight with them and

the locals. Other than this general advice of

what I would do I can't give you much more

than a warning of the area. It is the most

dangerous area to get the gold but if you want

to win big and win often it's the place to be.

Next we take our focus to the South

America's in Peru. Gold mining there is a toxic

legacy to the community. They all want to hit it

big but in the process they destroy themselves

and the community. There is a ton of mercury in

the area and by searching for the gold they stir

up all this mercury into the water. They then

buy and eat fish to survive and are all getting

sick. If you are going to be searching for gold in

the area just avoid the fish and don't drink the

water! Just stick to the local McDonalds. The

one time I went treasure finding in Peru I ate

only McDonalds. When you're in the big city

you buy as much water and McDonalds as

possible. I would typically run into the city once

a week and fill my whole truck up with

McDonald's big macs. McDonalds has so many

preservatives in the food it's like beef jerky and

never goes bad! One thing you can possibly

develop from mining in Peru is possibly

developing a super power from all the mercury

exposer. I have been watching a lot of these

new superhero movies and according to these

movies you can sometimes gain a superpower

when coming in contact with a very high level of

things like poison or gamma rays. Now I don't

know about you but even if you don't find gold I

would still consider a new super power

"treasure" so cross your fingers and hell, eat all

that fish and drink the local water if you want

maximum exposure. One thing I can't stress

enough and may seem random is to tip the

Peruvian flute bands on the streets. These local

bands bring great luck to your venture but you

only gain the luck if you tip them. As the show

South Park has shown us, they keep the world

safer than we all knew.

Lastly let's talk about what most of you will have the most access to, the North West of the United States of America. Like I talked about in the chapter "Right Under Your Nose" we all know there is tons of loot hidden away all over America as well as plenty of gold in the Northwest and even a few antiques and artifacts. Unlike all the other places I have mentioned America is actually somewhat safe compared to these third world countries. Don't

let your guard completely fall aside though,

there are still plenty of dangers among the old

west. If you're American the first thing I

suggest is getting your concealed weapons

permit and packing some heat. Half the time

they come in sue when you run into some gold

digging biker gang like the gang "Heavens

Devils" which is the Hells Angels rival gang. The

Heavens Devils are huge in treasure hunting

and are mostly found panning for gold. If you run into them on their turf insure you deeply apologize and get out! But the other half the time you need to be packing heat is for grizzly's and wild dingo's. An arsenal I would suggest to put together would be the following. A double barrel shotgun, an AR15, 50 caliber handgun, a katana, a bazooka, flashbang grenades and smoke bombs. If you can fit more into your rig please so but what I listed are the bare minimum basics for tackling treasure hunting in

America. Now if you're going to be panning for

gold you will want to focus on Washington,

Oregon and the north half of California starting

just below San Francisco. Those gold coins

found in a can I referenced earlier, that was

around San Francisco. Now I'm not going to try

to tell you panning techniques in a book, that

would be a waste of time. Go to our beloved

friend YouTube and research panning

techniques yourself. One quick rookie mistake is the pan color you use. You want something that will make the gold stick out so my suggestions are green, blue and my favorite black. But another big tip is to own a bright yellow one to loan to your friends and family. You don't want them getting your gold! Panning is a great way to find the gold in the ol west but I have actually made more money off finding jewelry in our American rivers. Think about it, us fat cat

Americans love to waist money in every way whether it's new clothes every month to keep up with the trends, nacho machines, glass knives from Mexico or my favorite, jewelry! A big ol hardened piece of carbon that shows our status and proves our love. Remember, the bigger the diamond the more that couple is in love. Now to find this jewelry in rivers you're not going to need a pan or a metal detector, in fact you're not going to believe where you're going to find it. Tourist river destinations where people tube down rivers. They rent a tube by the hour, hike to the top of the river and jump in going down the river over rapids and smaller waterfalls. While going over these 1-4 foot waterfalls everyone falls over in the river. Adrenalins pumping, your knees are knocking around on all the rocks and you usually come out bleeding. Many tourists also come out without their jewelry! Boo ya and sign me up!

It's not like there is a lost and found to return

that damn thing so finders keepers. I was on a

monster truck circuit in 2014 and we visited this

smaller town in Idaho. While there I did some

quick research to find treasure like always and

found this place 45 miles away called Lava Hot

Springs. Tons of people float this river right

through the city and sure enough the daredevils

go off some 3-4 ft waterfalls and get worked. I

had bought a snorkel from Walmart and found

3 diamond rings in the river just below that waterfall. You do need to know technique on where to look and understand the water flow. There are usually a few hotspots where most things like jewelry will flow into and when you find those you cash out! The picture on the cover of this book is from that river dive!

Although South Africa and South Australia are the best places to find gold American is still great for gold, jewelry and fallout shelters.

Panning For Gold

I want to insure I go over a few important facts

about panning for gold I haven't hit on yet. There

are different levels of gold panners. I myself am

rated at P90 so I know a thing or two. I already

talked about tactics on color of pans and what to

give your friends but now let's really take an inside

look. First off lets good at some facts, 20 million

ounces of river gold were found in California rivers

during the gold rush so let's understand this isn't

going to come easy. All the easy stuff was taken off

the surface so were going to have to work for it.

First you search your river until you find those black

sands which is the best clue to where the gold is.

Next we know all the easy stuff has been found so

it's time to have some fun. Chipping hammers are

for chumps, use dynamite and bombs! Yes you read

right, we're going to harness our inner 14 year old

but instead of making little bombs out of fireworks

and playing with firecrackers were going to go big!

Pipe bombs, dynamite, grenades, anything you can

get your hands on to give mother nature a good ol

anal probe right up her river system! But Matt,

that's illegal, isn't it? Shut the hell up and light the

fuse! Hey if you want to get rich you gotta bend a

few rules and take some risks. Rules were made to be broken. I'm not going to tell you specifics how to build a pipe bomb but we all know... usually a little galvanized pipe with caps, some black powder, a long fuse and a hole drilled in one end for our fuse and boom! Literally boom, were rich and were gonna have fun doing it. Besides let's remember what George Washington said, "America was founded on beer, pizza, guns, and homemade pipe bombs!"

Now let's talk on finding the right blast zone.

Ancient river beds where the water has lowered is

where many gold deposits are found! Rounded

boulders are proof there was once a river and gold

is often close. If you cannot determine areas of

ancient rivers use the inside bends of the river with

its sluggish flow is where we find our fortune. I

usually like to plant my bomb 2 feet under the

ground and let her rip! Go pan in the new hole of

your blast zone where nobody has ever been before

and get ready to buy some new jet skis with all that

cash! If a tree falls in a forest with NOBODY around

does it make a sound? If I have fun with dynamite

out in the forest when NOBODY is around, is it

illegal? I say no. You have now created a gold mine!

Metal Detectors

Metal detectors are one of the most common

ways people hunt for treasure and often call

themselves detectorists. If you think detectorists

are a joke or waste of time let me tell you a little

secret right away. The largest gold nugget ever

found at 75 troy ounces was with a metal

detector and it was buried just 12 inches

underground! Read this chapter, follow my tips,

get pumped up and start maxing out those credit

cards cuz we're gonna be rich bitch!

Now don't get me wrong you still need to do

your research. If there is one thing I can't say

enough it's research research RESEARCH! With

metal detecting you're not usually looking for

gold nuggets but more for gold coins and long lost

treasure of ancient kings. My greatest find was in

Danbury near London. It was an old gold artifact

from lost kings and it now sits in the natural

history museum in London. That's not what

important about this artifact, what I need to warn

you all about is the curse of the gold. Many lost

artifacts and treasure are known to be cursed

which is what us treasure hunters refer to as "The

curse of the gold". Curses come in many different

ways and with this piece it's the only one I

noticeably have found myself and recognized the

curse. After finding my piece of history I suddenly couldn't find anything with my metal detector. No junk, no matchbox cars, not even a tin can. This is when I realized I was cursed. After visiting and investigating the museum and my piece I soon realized I could not steal it back. I was desperate as I knew I would never find treasure again with this curse. The museum had valued my piece at 50k which I got half and the other half went to the landowner. (When detecting always split your winning with a landowner if they gave you

permission on their land or you're insured a

curse) Now I need to end this curse and I couldn't

get my gold back to put it back so I had to figure

this out. I can't guarantee what I did will work for

all of you but I spend my complete 25k on gold

coins. I then went back to a nearby field from my

dig site and simply buried my gold back into

mother earth. Instantly I could hear the birds, I

could smell the ocean, I could feel the wind. I had

beaten the curse.

Now with metal detecting you don't want to be

messing around. Don't buy some power ranger

metal detector from a pawn shop, you need the

best money can buy. Now if you don't have the guts

to sell your kidney (you literally already have one

kidney and cannot sell one) then another part of

your body you and sell is your plasma. This stuff is

liquid gold! Find a local plasma dealer and start

giving, a couple months later you will have your

detector and you will have all your research done

for your new career as a detectorist. My personal

favorite detector is the Minelab BPZ 7000 but I also

power it with a car battery for extra juice. If I want

to I can find gold over 300 ft under the earth! But if

you're just getting started and you're too scared to

have a powerful detector you will be fine with a

Garrett Ace 150 for the first few months.

There is real danger with being a detectorist!

My buddie Terry runs a detectorist club called the

DMDC and while digging up a find he hit a land mine

and was thrown 40+ft! He was lucky he didn't lose

any limbs but many do. One detectorist lost all 4

limbs and is now called Nubs. She actually had a

song written about her by her favorite band NOFX

call "she's nubs" be sure to check it out. My point is

that you will want to wear some body armor and a

bullet proof jacket at all times just in case.

Ever hear that saying "bury me with my money"?

That's because it's what everyone did in the old

days both ancient and even cowboys within the last

couple hundred years. All the money is 6ft deep

waiting to be found! Back then plenty of money was

still in the form of gold and silver so it's time to start

digging! Research is easy on this one, you search

the name, find someone with historic riches and go!

Use your detector and look for the goods 4-6 feet

down. If cops ever catch you in the act you simple

need to explain you are part of a ghost hunting

reality tv show that will be airing in a few months.

Pass your metal detector off as a type of spirit

reader. Everyone has been captured with these

series and the last thing they want to do is disrupt

what's soon to be their favorite show. If this doesn't

work it's a perfect opportunity to try out those

military grade smoke bombs and flash bangs we got

off the black market right!

DB Cooper

If you don't know who DB Cooper is then you're a

rookie and need to get it together. My Grandpa was

DB Coopers mentor and I know all the details how

he got away with it that has never been shared. I

won't be surprised when the FBI is trying to

questions me for more info after reading this but I'm going all out for my readers. Many treasure hunters have searched and search for his 200K in cash and have never found it. They never found his body, the money or his parachute. That's because he was a genius and I'm about to tell you how he did it. These days his plan never would have worked with all the technology and resources but back in 1971 it was no problem. In 1971 everyone was busy still tripping from Woodstock in 69 and dropping acid to care about aviation security. You may be

thinking 200k isn't that much but back in 1971 that

was equivalent to 1.2M with today's inflation.

Like we know he high jacked a plane in Seattle,

demanded 200K in cash and some parachutes. They

take off and 45 min later he jumps. From here

nobody knows what happened but I do. He lands on

NW Hayes rd in Hayes Washington. There he has his

friend Hank the garbage man waiting for him. He

dumps his chute in the garbage truck to never be

found again and gets a ride to Lake Merwin. He pays

off his friend Hank with 50 bucks and a case of

Pabst Blue Ribbon beer. He then hops in my

grandpas seaplane which was a Piper PA-18 Super

Cub with a big bore kit and nitrous for hairy

situations. They both then fly into Seattle, he gives

my grandpa 4K and leaves. When my grandpa asked

what he would do next he said he would be

investing all his money in worm farms in Argentina.

Legend has it he was broke by 1992 and now hunts

for treasure like the rest of us. I tell you this story

for one simple reason, don't waste your time

looking for this lost treasure.

Family Vacations

When most people imagine their vacations they

imagine things like eating all the new and exciting

food, days on the beach, roller coasters, Disney or

maybe just sitting in a hot tub soaking it up with

their soul mate. Not me. When you say vacation I see a new opportunities to get rich quick! I see an opportunity to leave on that vacation on credit and come back with possibly millions! Vacations are one of the most underrated ways to get out and find treasure!

First you need to plan the vacation and see what's in your budget or where you can get before maxing out that master card. Are we going to go camp alongside some rivers in California or are we going to the Bahamas which will make the family

happy and also just so happens to be within 40

miles of three or more pirate ship wrecks? These

vacation spots may be the biggest decision of your

life and you need to go prepared. Take what tools

and equipment you can and plenty of cash to pay

off the locals when it comes to rides, scuba gear or

just info alone.

One topic most treasure authors avoid talking

about is family. Their cowards and for both our

sakes I'm going to go there. I'm going to say what were all thinking. Can you trust your family? When you find that 10 troy oz nugget how do you know any one of them won't take it and flee to Cabo? All I'm saying is it may be smart to hire a lawyer to get some legal documents together which the family needs to sign. Generally in the treasure community a fair deal is that you get to keep 75% of all findings and the rest will be divided to the family. It sounds crazy right? It's not and I have even seen some treasure hunters go north of 90%! Just insure you think this over and get the best lawyer in town. It may cost a couple grand now for their services but you'll be thanking me when you find the gold.

Now what if your family is completely trustworthy and in it to win it just like you. We consider yourself lucky and let's examine how you can work as a family to get maximum results. First off how young is too young? My great great great grandad had my great great grand dad panning for

11 hour shifts by his 3rd birthday, but that was a

different day back then. Now I would say it's socially

acceptable to be working those kinds of shifts by

age 5. You need to use the children to your full

advantage. Their favorite tv shows should be these

gold mining shows. They will be very smart in

science and geology class. They should be learning

to read with this book you're reading now. Have as

many children as possible and before you know it

you will have a 15 man workforce. What many

treasure hunters run into is picking the best ones to

go on vacation when you can only fit a certain

amount in the van. I'll let you do the ranking

research on your own and find the best ways to

only pick your best to go on the vacations with you.

Learn it, Live it, Find it

Now that you have more details on how, when

and where to find treasure it's time to get a plan

together. Like the title says you first need to learn it.

You need to learn the good spots around your area.

We don't have thousands of dollars to waste

traveling far just to search for treasure. If you do

have an interesting spots somewhat close you may

be able to take advantage of planning family

vacations around the area which we already talked

about. Learning your area may not be as hard as

you think. First there is obviously a quick google

search that can do you wonders and may even

report what others have found. Often people who

find the mother load want to keep those spots

private since everyone wants to get theirs. Still, do

the research on any finds in your area. Make sure

you also search the traits of your area. Was there

mining in the past? What is generally found in your

soil? Do others participate in finding any types of

treasure?

One of the best ways to get to know your area

is through the locals. Look on Facebook and

perhaps there is a treasure finding group in your

area that gets together to share techniques and

spots. With these groups insure you are very

careful. They may seem to be your friends but I

insure you they're not! These groups are like pirates

and are always out to get a share of your finds.

Some groups even have waivers to sign where they

share findings or are required to give a percentage

of any findings if over a certain amount. Avoid these

groups of filthy animals at all costs. If you are going

to join a group insure it's free and do it with the

mind set of "know the enemy". That's right, enemy.

Anyone out there looking for the gold will stab you

in the back the first chance they get. Get in with the

group to get any possible intel on the area. Any past

finds? Any proven spots? Groups can also be a good

resource to learn certain skills like proper metal

detector use or spots in the river where you look for

gold flow. Have you ever heard of people hiring

native American hunting guides for those huge

hunts where they get the biggest 30 point bucks?

Why not research any native trackers for treasure

as well? They are in tune with mother nature and

the spirit of the gold. I once hired a native American

tribe member out of the San Francisco bay area for twenty bucks. We didn't find any gold that day but while walking back to the car from our gold panning session we came across a hundred dollar bill in the campsite parking lot. Now tell me that's not in tune with mother nature! This type of research is the first thing you need to start considering before you waste any more of your precious time...

Live it. Only the most successful treasure hunters strike it rich and they don't do it by playing patty cake with their friend Pedro. They do it by living the lifestyle and becoming fully emerged in the hunt. Life is treasure hunting and treasure hunting is life. You know you'll be a successful treasure hunter when you can't sleep and you're going on midnight excursions. You will be selling your plasma twice a week just to stay up on the newest model of metal detectors. You will be out camping for weeks at a time using all your PTO while digging holes two stories deep. You will be in great shape because you will always be on the

move so there will be no need for a gym. You may

even find jobs that are only seasonal so you can

then treasure hunt full time the other half the year

in Peru only drinking goat milk and eating wild

berries off the land like one of my buddy Emilio. He

works his summers as a wildland firefighter for the

Bureau of Land Management on a hotshot crew.

Then all winter he lives in Peru substituting

deodorant with a crystal he rubs on his armpits and

lives the hunt. To this day Emilio has found a total

of .5 ounces of gold which he lost that night

gambling but he knows the next big nugget is just

around the next river bend.

Find it. Now that you have read my book you

have the upper ground on all the other bozo's out

there just wasting their lives away. Posers who

don't know the half it. People who haven't even

found a single flake yet probably believe they are

qualified to give advice... Be wary of these people

and their advice, they may be just around the bend.

If you are reading this now you are at the end of my

book which means you are no poser. By reading this

book alone it qualifies you to increase one full

treasure band ranking. If your ranking was a T-100

you are now a T-200. If you were already maxed out

at a T-800 you are now a T-800+. Consider yourself

a professional and start acting like one. Good luck

and may the gold be ever in your favor.

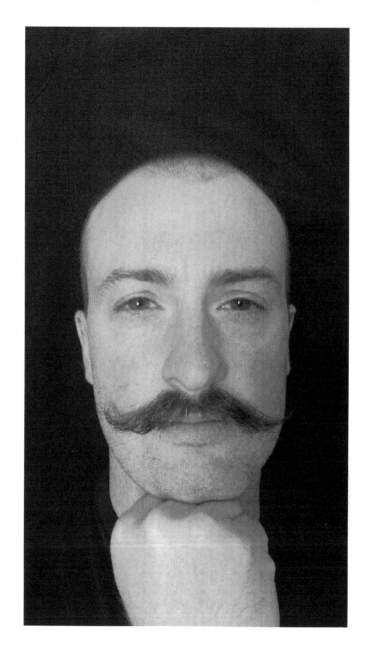

I dedicate this book to my mustache